PIRATES UNCORRUPTED
Art and story by: Seraphina T. Harbinger

Typeface: Quicksand
Designed by: Andrew Paglinawan
Published in: 2011

This is a work of fiction, resemblences to
names, places or persons,
living or otherwise, are coincidence
or used in a fictitious manner.

See the authors other work at:
https://www.pinterest.com/
High_Empress_Of_Coconutia/

https://www.youtube.com/channel/
UCCFM6B6FSYaNfRbodMgxoQw

...

I said I
was sorry.

...

Please talk
to meeee!

Pleeeeeease

Ugh!
"Dont worry about the ship," you said.
"I'll handle it," you said.
"You just worry about getting supplies," you said.
I did say that...

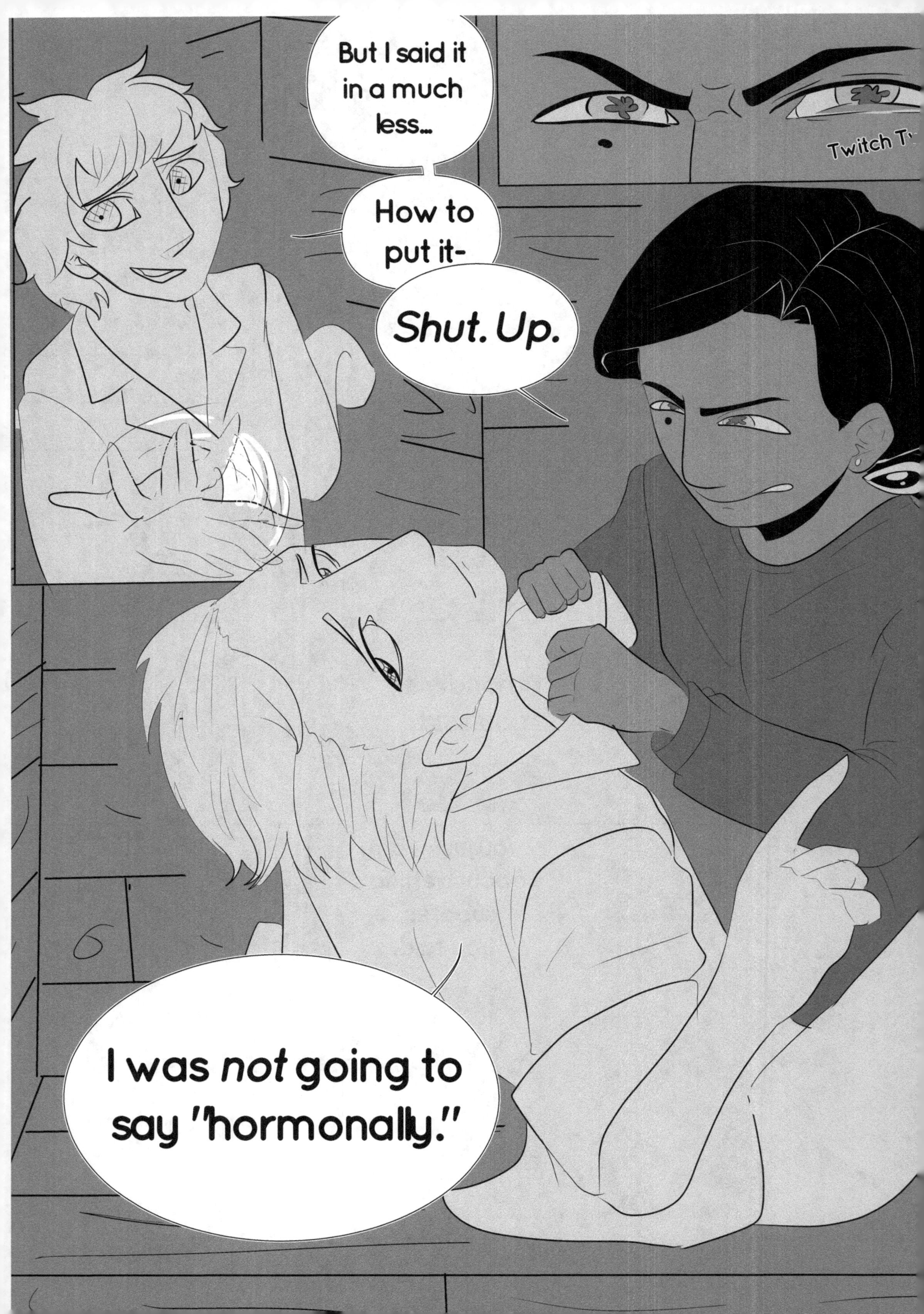

But I said it in a much less...
How to put it-
Shut. Up.
I was not going to say "hormonally."

Goddamn pirates, Jasper!
We stowed away on a pirate ship!
Yes we did...

And what did you want me to do?
Walk up to them and say:

"Hi,
My friend and I would like to stow away on this fine ship of yours...
...and would like to clarify that you are not, in fact, pirates."

Or necromancers, or cannibals, or-
-Or spherical connoisseurs whose dealings are with eyes.
Yes, yes!
Let's not focus too much on mistakes of the past,
And instead, look forward to tomorrow!

At least we made it a few days without getting caught this time.
Ugh

I am sorry for knocking that container on your head though...
And I did try to hold in that sneeze.
Ohmygodshutu
Creeeeeeeak

What?

Creeeak

Someone's coming.

Click
Hurry up!

Who...
...Are you?

Pantaloon Cobbler and Jojoarina!
...Okay...
Why are you on our ship?
Sightseeing.

What is your reference, port, or starboard plank?
Our preference is none.

Tell us who you are, real[ly]
I told you, we're sightseeing.

Yeah...
That doesn't *really* help your friend here, now does it.

Either I learn the name of a live ma
or a dead one.
Your choice.

Fine, my name is Lady Lucea Tuum II.
The little fellow you're threatening is my entourage, Sir Jasper Stultus.

Tuum?
If you're a
Lady,
how did you
end up on
our ship?

...After parting company with my father, the sir and I were set to traverse on a passenger ship...
Unfortunately, we were purloined by street ruffians.

They separated us from our personal belongings, and as such, we ended up stowing away on this fine ship.

So...
you ran away
from home,
Then,
got robbed.
And that's how
you ended up
stowed away on
our ship.
NODS
OHH.
Yes.

What Family did you say you were part of?
Tuum...
Uh huh.
Psst, Capitain.
tug
Yes?
The Tuum family is pretty obscure,
Most normal peasants wouldn't know about them.

money?
If they're telling the truth, there may be money there.
So, how much can we ransom them for?
Emi,
What?
We're about to find out.

Who would
pay ransom
for you?

Telling you
that would
certainly defeat
the purpose
of running away
now wouldn't
it?

Oh?

You wanna
rethink that?

Fine.

Just let us
keep our
heads.

You may contact Captain Jonothan Tuum,
Tell him you've captured his "darling pumpkin," and he'll know exactly of whom you're refering.
. . .

Well?
Hard to say,
Jonothan Tuum is a real person,
But he's had more wives, children, and mistresses than even he can keep track of.

I think we should give it a try.
What's the worst that happens?

I can think of a few ...
We're running low on money,
And we need repairs.
Don't forget about food.

I'm willing to risk it.
I'm sure Hop and Pearl are too.
Sigh

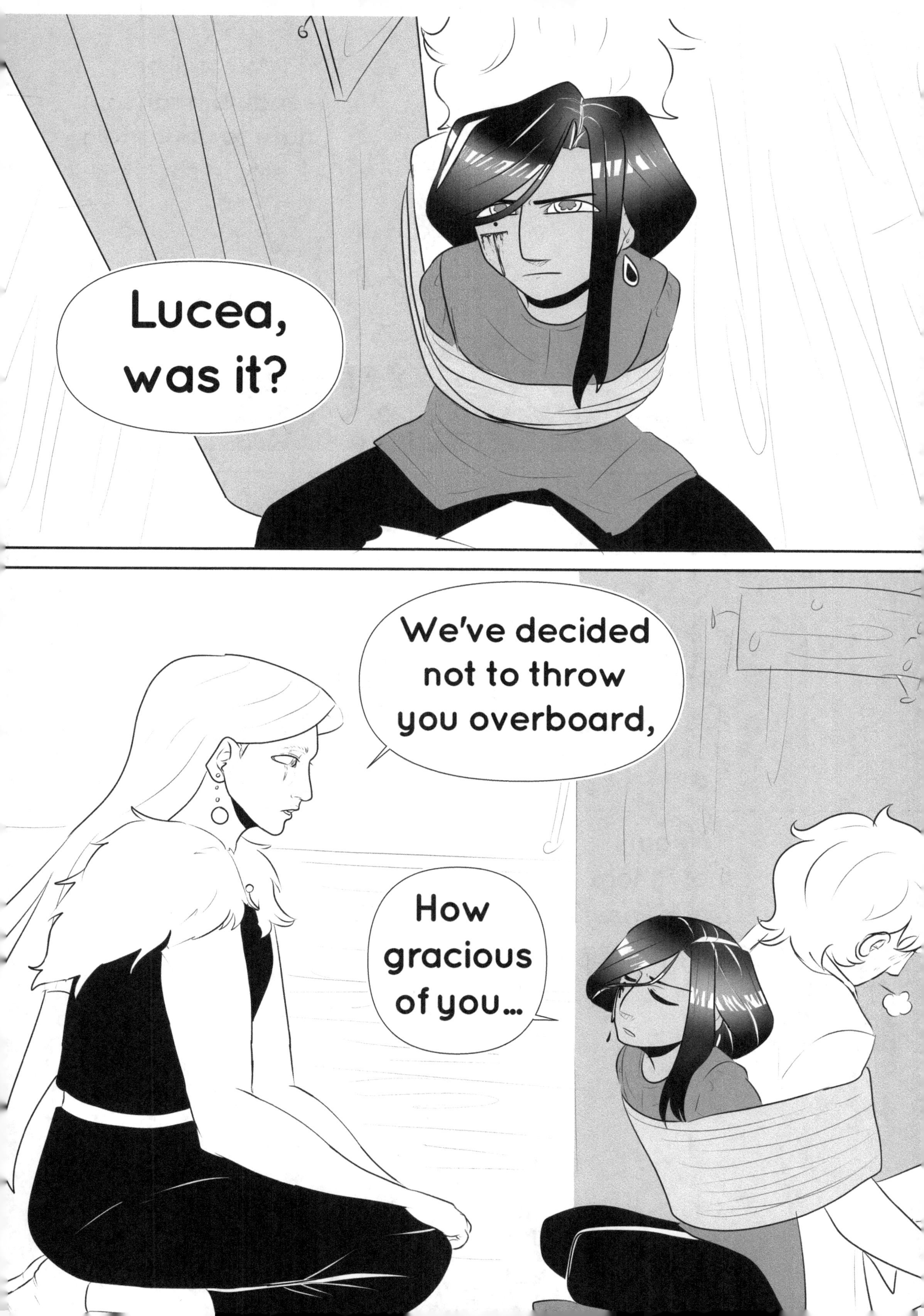

Lucea, was it?
We've decided not to throw you overboard,
How gracious of you...

From here on, you and your guard are our hostages.
We will be sending a ransom note to your main estate shortly,
Any questions?
Good.
Noemi, show them to our finest closet please.
Right-o.

This way, this way.
Do you have my ribbon?
Yeah.
Johann, here's the ain estate?
Around the Schads area.
SCHADS

Mister Hopkin, change course to Schads!
Pearl, see if there is anyone in that area who can deliver our ransom note for us!
Aye!
Right!
-Sigh-
Sometimes I wish wisdom really did come with age...

Pirates Uncorrupted

Attention!
So tall!
Yeah.

Ahem!
While you are on this ship, you will be cooking, and cleaning, and anything else that is asked of you,
Is that clear?

Ooh, the sail is super full now, huh?
Yeah...
Twtich
Twitch
Hey,
Crash!

Good luck!
It always turns out something like this doesn't it,

My Lady.
I'm going to smack you.
Captain,
Fwip
Fwip
The ransom note was delivered!

Excellent,
please inform me when we have a trade date.
Aye.
Mister Hopkin
What is our estimated arriv time?
About two days.

Good!
Johann,
When will lunch be ready?
Soon, Captain.
Fantastic!

Keep up the good work everyone!
Oh!
Where is Grigii?
Have you tried my belongings; You can usually find him there.

Or better yet,
Tie something shiny to a fishing line and draw him out.
That last part was uncalled for,
He's not a fish.
I'd certainly like to make him aquatic.

I think I heard him creeping around in storage.
You know,
For Pirates, they seem...

...Not evil?
Good and evil are man-made constructs.
ut no two eople are he same,
Which means no two goods, nor evils, will be the same.

You're getting too philisophical for me, Forts.
Hey!
I hear a lot of talking, but not a lot of swabbing!

How?
...e's like, ... feet in the air.
I have impeccable hearing!
Swab!
Swab!
Swab!
Swab!

BAM
I've been summoned by the taunting.
Swab!
Swab!
Swab!
Swab!

Ring
Ring
Ring

Food's
ready!

Are you
two coming?

This is one of those rhetorical questions, isn't it
Suspicious much?
We just weren't expecting it...
Most people don't ask their hostages to eat with them,
Unless they want something...

So,
What do you want?
What?
You've been working in the sun all day on an empty stomach,
and it's currently late lunch-early dinner time.
Hot
Hot
Hot
Hot
ON!
grow,
Clean Clean
Clean
Hungry Cleaning
&
Sparkle
MOPPING!
Hangry MOPPING! MOPPING!

You may be hostages, but we're not monsters.

But I can see that your biases against my profession of choice over-shadow my individual character...

So,

I can work with that...

If you really want me to be a monster,

CRACK
CRACKLE
CRACK

NOW GET YER BUTTS BELOW DECK AND JOIN ME FOR LATE-LUNCH/ EARLY DINNER OR ELSE!
Yessir...
And so they did.

Pirates Uncorrupted

You know,
There are a lot of different kinds of people onboard.
Yeah.

I've never seen a giant before the captain.
Yeah.
I wonder what the cat-person is.
Dunno.

I'm pretty sure the angry red-head is a vampire.
Yeah.
How are we oing to handle the trade off?
I don't know.

We'll figure it out,
We still have time.
They really didn't.

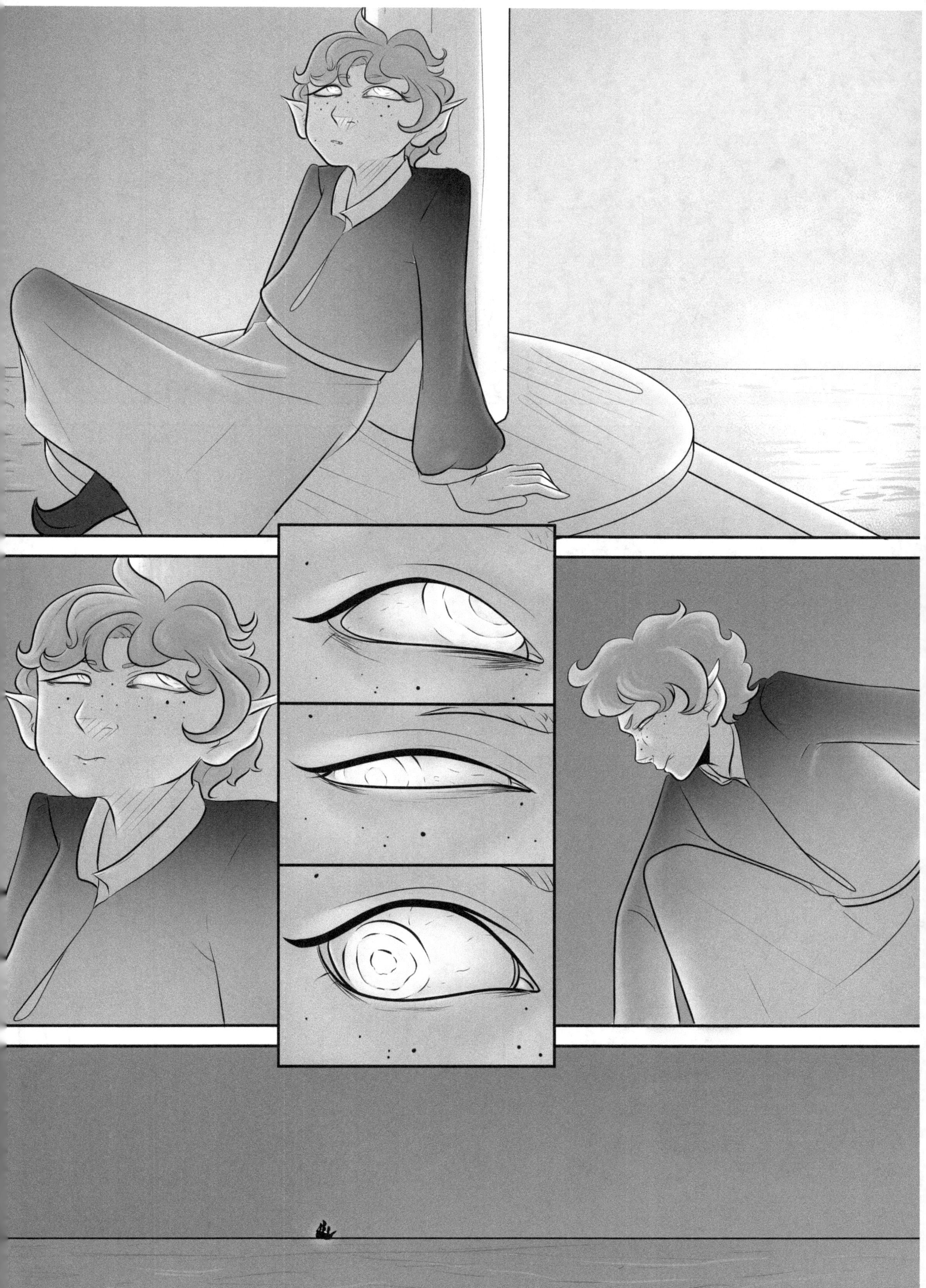

uugh

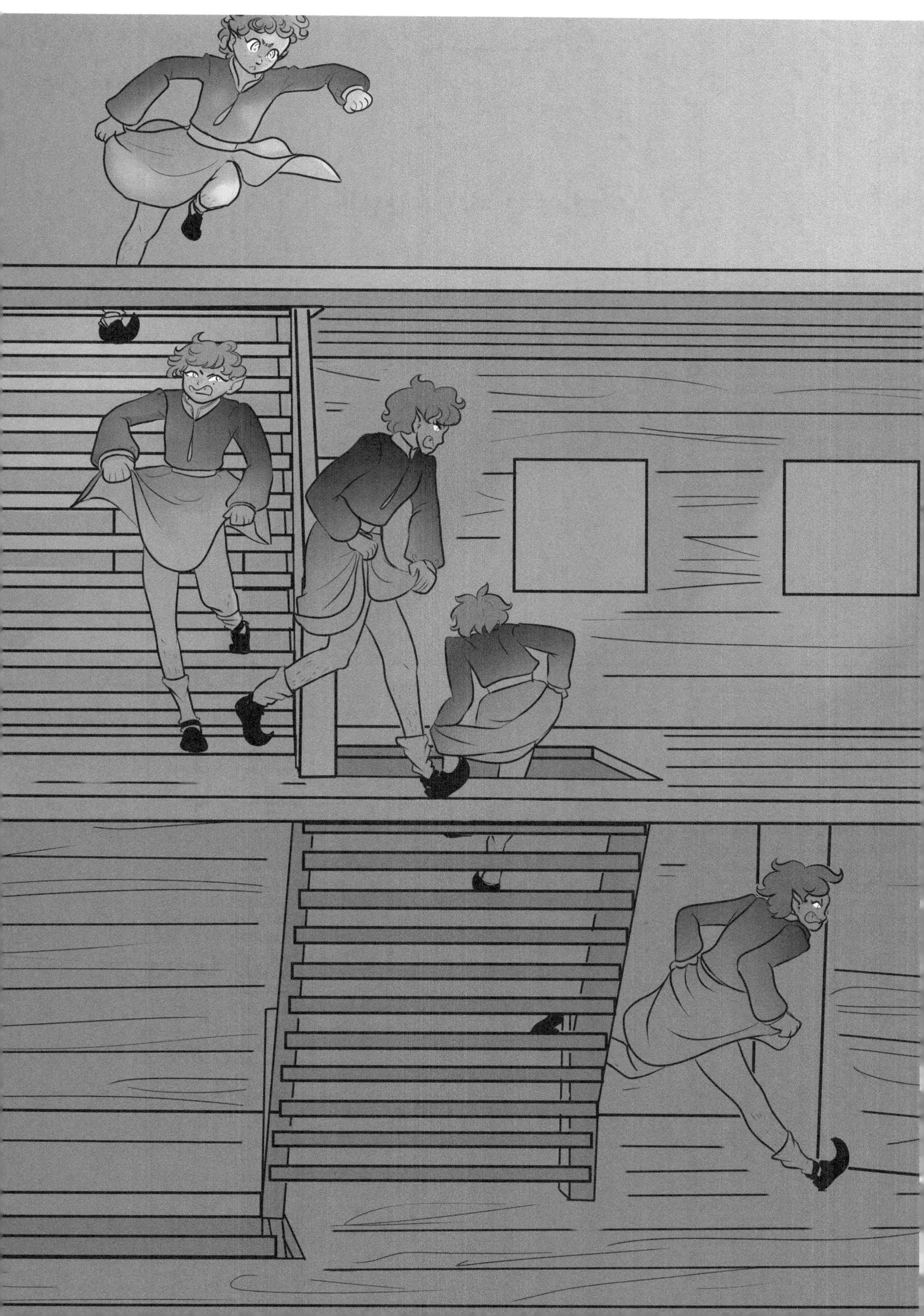

Everyone need to wake up!
Wakey wakey!!!
If you don't get your tired behinds out of bed right now I will set your blankets on fire!

What's going on?
There's a military ship at our 8:00.
What!
Damn it, they're early!
Aye.
Hop, man the wheel!
Miz Pearl, start waking the captain!

Miz Emi, you're in charge until the captain's on deck.
Aye.
Captain!
Captain!
Wake up captain!!!

Miz Pearl,
Use the big guns.

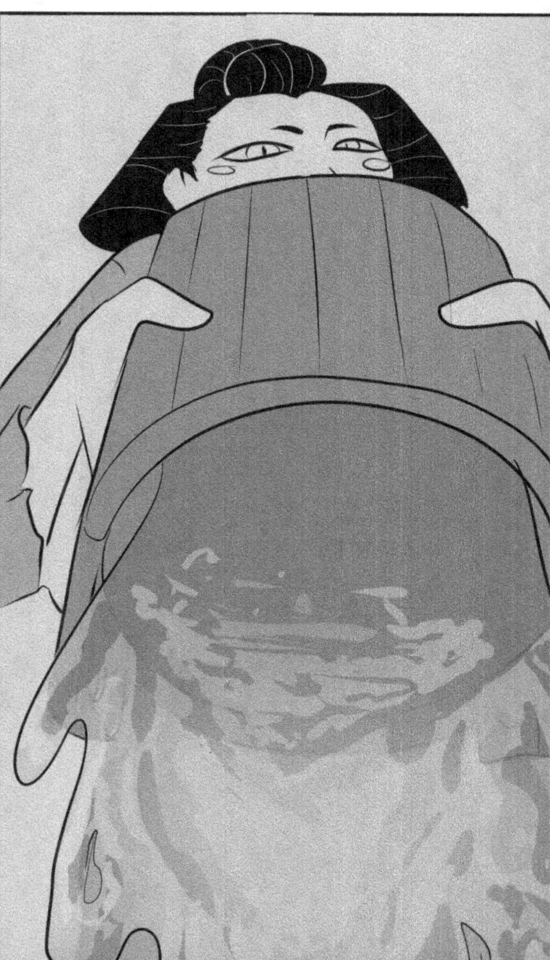

What!!!
What's going on!!!
Is there a leak?
Are we sinking?
Where's Grigii?
There's a ship getting awful close to us, Captain,
We figured you might like to be awake for when we make our exchange.

What?!

Everyone
to your
stations!!!

Oh...
Johann, is there any chance we have coffee?
I'll go make some now.
Thank you!

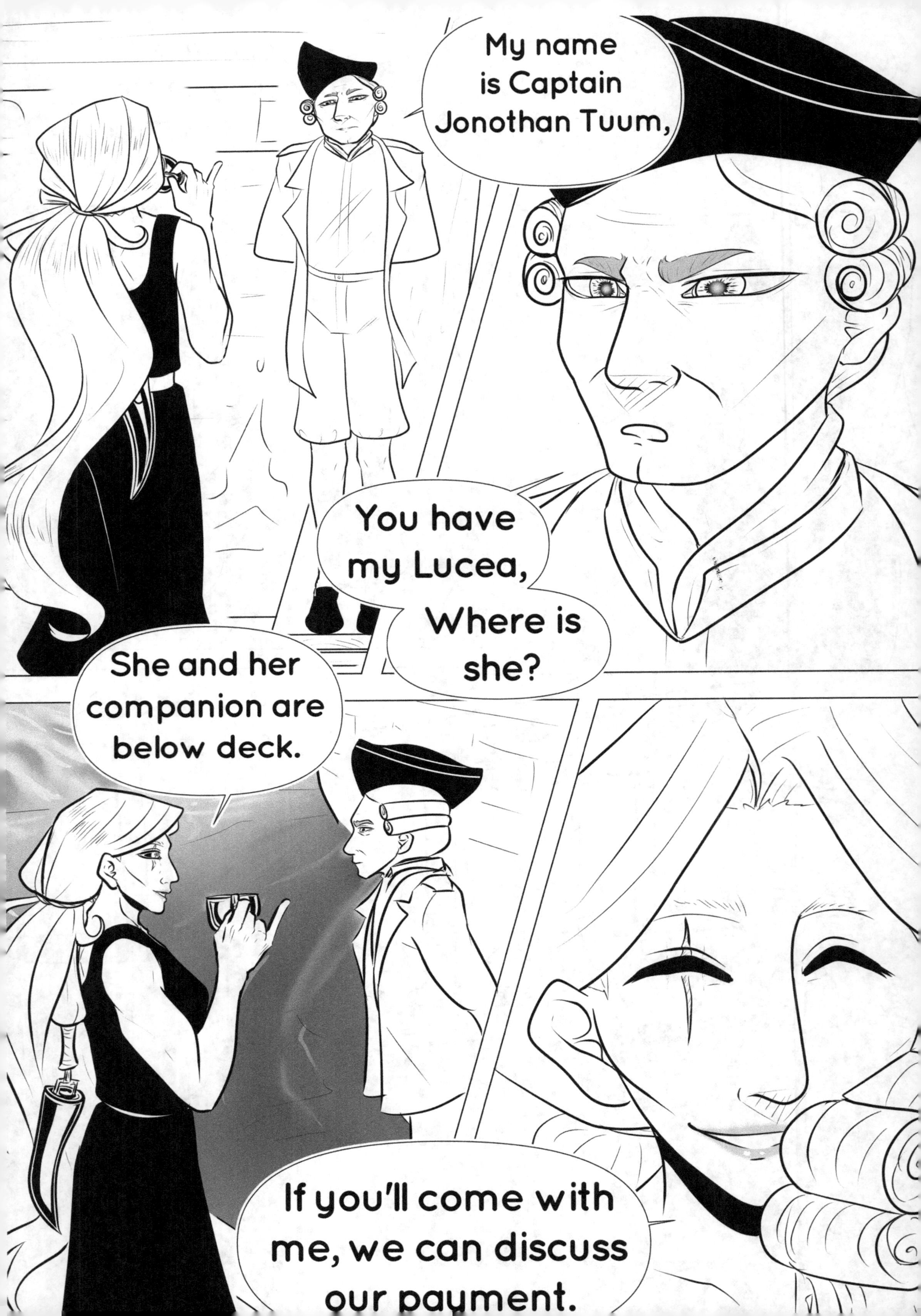

My name is Captain Jonothan Tuum,
You have my Lucea, Where is she?
She and her companion are below deck.
If you'll come with me, we can discuss our payment.

No!
We do this right here.
Very well.
Here sir.
Good lad.
Hmm
Rustle Rustle
Is this it?

Show me
my daughter!
Noemi, if
you please.

Ugh, it's
too bright.
Hehehe.

Pumpkin?

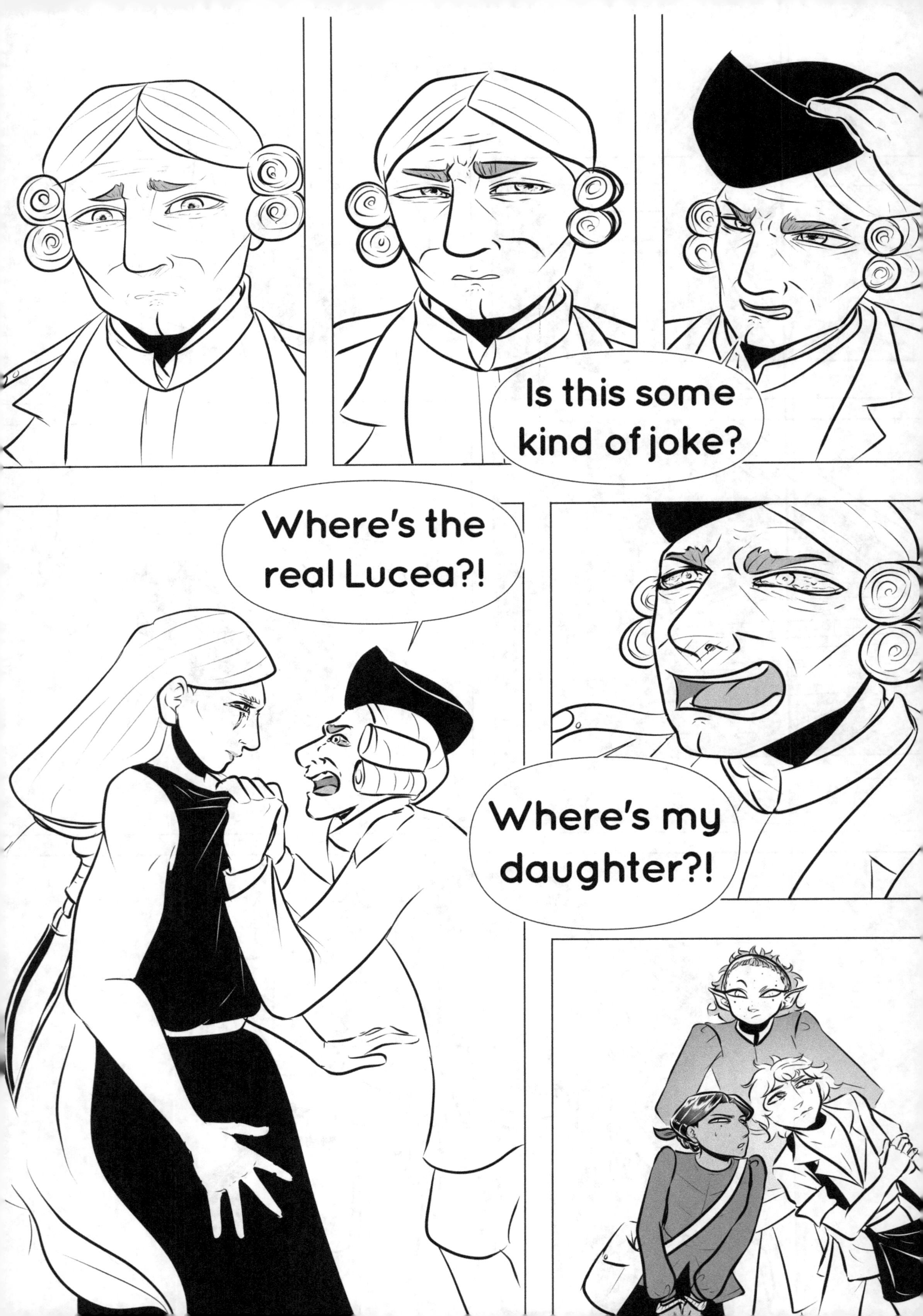

Is this some kind of joke?
Where's the real Lucea?!
Where's my daughter?!

Wha-

Sorry!

Men,
Get them!

Click

Hurry!

You little-
SHIIIITS!!!

I'll punch you all the way back into your mother's womb and dance on her grave!!!
Emi...
That hurt!
Both physically and emotionally!

Noemi, Focus.
ow ow ow ow ow ow
I was actually starting to like you!
And remember not to kill anyone.
I know goddamn it.
Honestly,
I'm not a chil

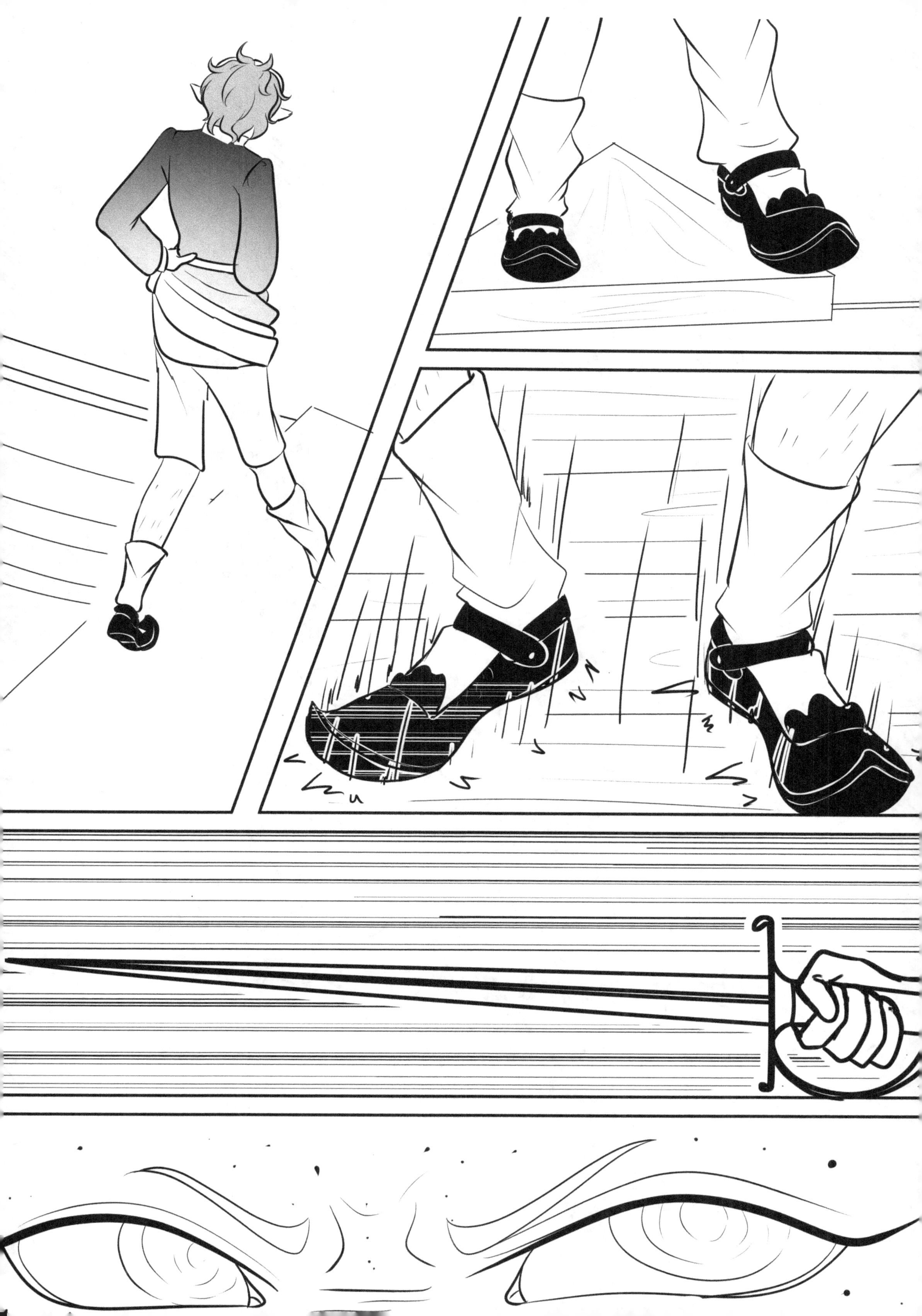

BANG
ow, Fuck!
Ptu

Click
Sploosh
Hey! That was my brothers' musket!
Um, sorry...?
Fwip
Agh! Emi, look out!
Gun!

BANG

CRASH
Ah.
Agh!

Let's clear out this entire fucking ship.
Non-fatally, of course.

Men,
Get to the
cannons!
You
can try.
Hiss
Rip .

Ugh!
Come on!
There has to be something of value down here!
SALTED PORK
Keep looking.
Isn't it a bit weird that there wasn't anyone below deck?
Considering how quickly they caught up to us, lack of men, and lack of provisions,

I'd assume they left while restocking or something.
That would explain why there's basically nothing down here.
Yeah...
tap
tap
tap
tap
tap tap
tap
tap
tap
tap
tap
tap
tap
I'm going to the kitchen.

I'll go to the quarters.
We can meet at the Captain's cabin.
CREEEEAK

What is it?
I don't know.
SALTED
PORK
Clatter
SALTED
PORK
Clink
Clink
Clatter

Hisssssss!
'♪ Hidey Ho,
time to go ♪
♪♪

SWIPE
Clatter
Crack
Shatter

Hmmm...
Rumble
On second thought,
Let's just head to the kitchen.
Yeah,
I really don't feel like putting my swimming skills to the test.

clink

grab
CRACK

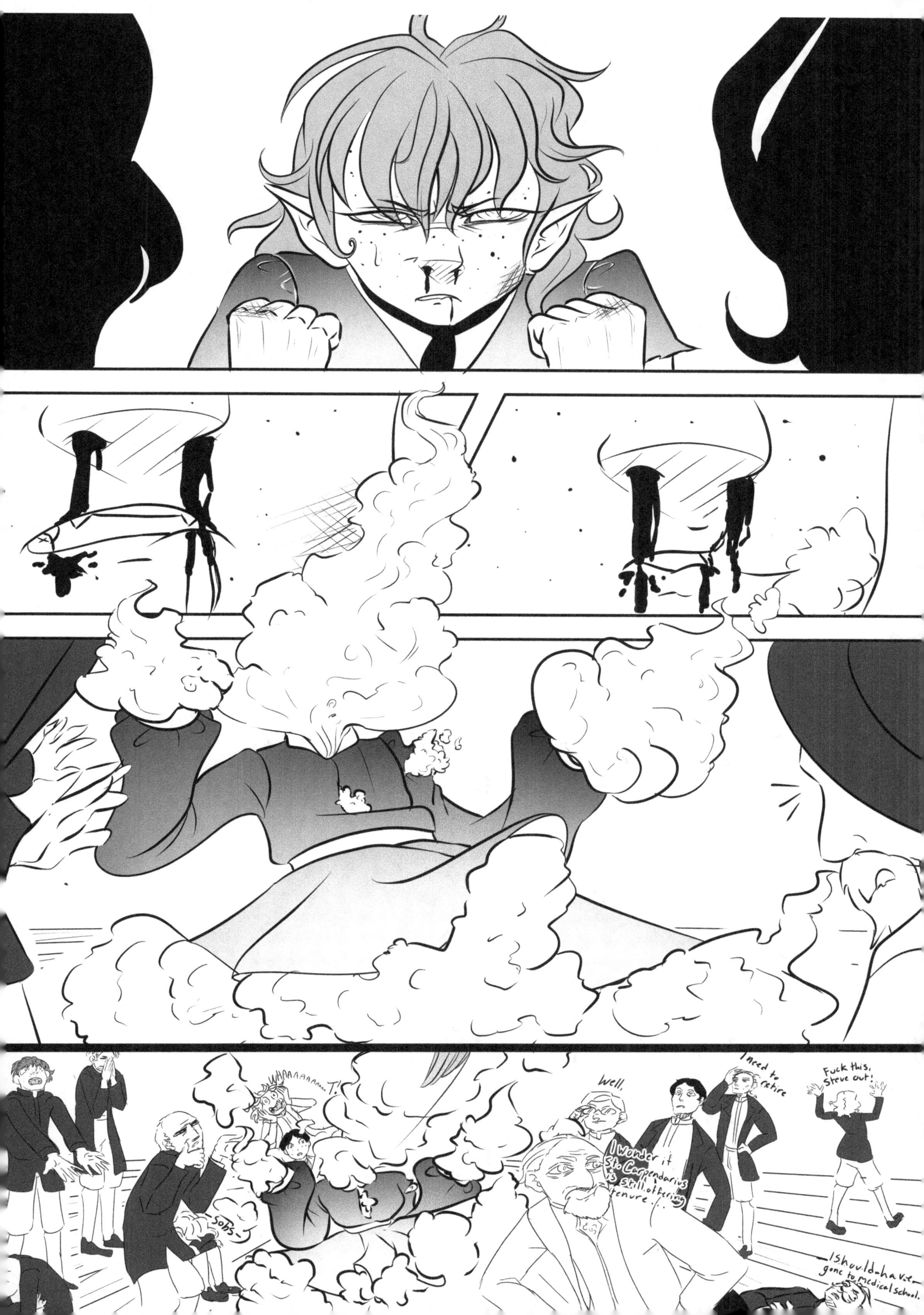

WHAAAAAAAAT!
sobs
Well,
I wonder if St. Carpendarius is still offering tenure...
I need to retire
Fuck this, Steve out!
I should have gone to medical school.

Anyone with ammo left, shoot the bird!
And where are my cannons!?

Sir, they've cut our anchor!
We have a spare, shoot the bird!
And get me my cannons!
Hop, the sails!

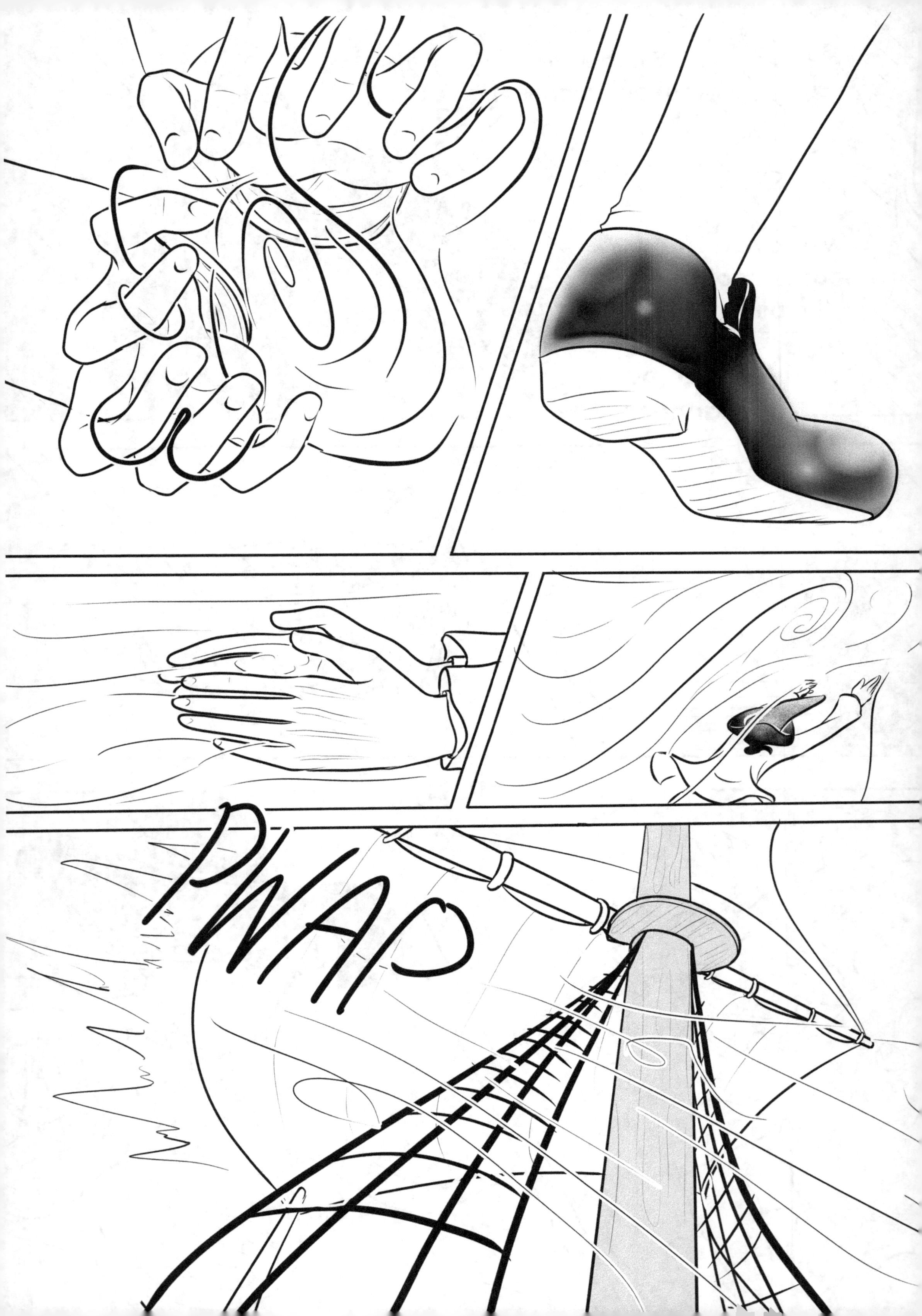
PWAP

WHERE ARE MY CANNONS!?
Well?
Egh...

Surrender, pirates!
Or I shoot the goblin!

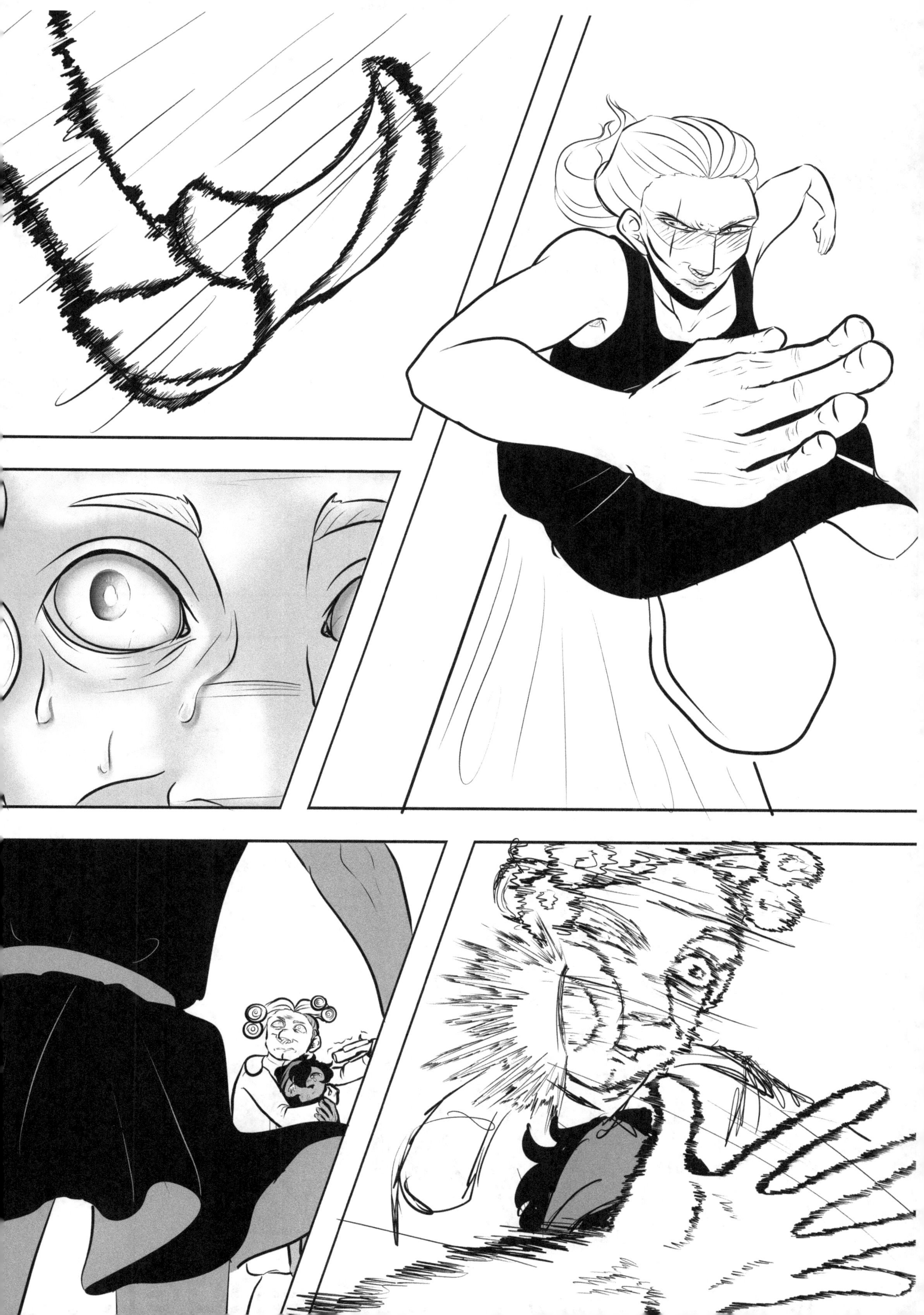

SWIPE
CRACK
No,
You surrender.

You should be greatful, Captain...
I could tear you limb from limb, and hang you with your own small intestine.
But I suppose then you'd never find your daughter.
Are you okay, Grigii?
Hmf.
Thank goodness.

Remember that we have talked about this, Grigorii,
you need to tell me before you go out.

Woo-hoo!
Anarchy!

Spltter

So,
Captain...

No.
I didn't even get to ask...
That was your "I want to set something on fire," tone.
Can I set them just a little bit on fire?
No,
We don't want to kill anyone.
Shwooooooooooooooooooo
CRASH

-Sigh-
You may throw ONE.
Yesssss.
NON-FATALLY!
I won't let you down, captain!
hehe
ARSON!!!

SHIT, Not again...
Pearl, I thought I said "non-fatally."
Meaning: they've at least some chance of survival.
Sorry, Captain.
This time it was an accident; I didn't adjust for the wind...
Hurry, men!
Get to the life-boats!

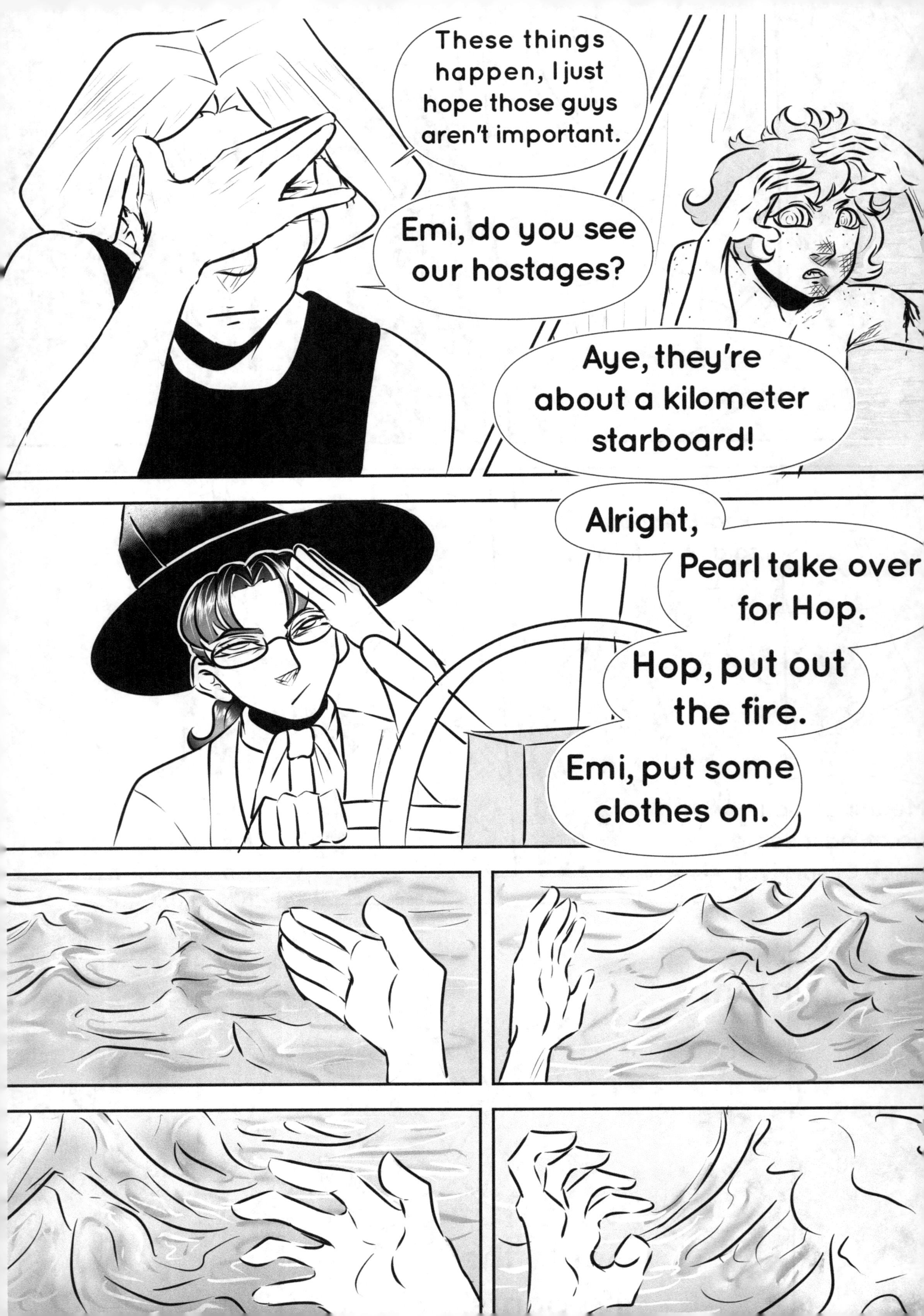

These things happen, I just hope those guys aren't important.
Emi, do you see our hostages?
Aye, they're about a kilometer starboard!
Alright, Pearl take over for Hop.
Hop, put out the fire.
Emi, put some clothes on.

If they drown on their own, it's not technically murder, right?
Yeah, that's sound logic.

Uh-oh...
Wha- oh?
Ugh.
Don't just gla
at it, row faste
twitch twitch

Need
a ride?
No thanks,
we're good!
Row,
Row!
Ah,
Do forgive
me,
That was
rhetorical
I believe
the word is
"Deja vu."

So,
I don't suppose you just wanted to check up on your old pals, huh?
No.
Well...
However,
Since we're a little short-staffed at the moment,
And you kind of owe us for that whole debacle,
We're offering an invitation to join our crew.
What.

"What" indeed, Captain.
Have you forgotten how they completely messed up my face?
Did you not threaten them with a meat cleaver?
I feel it was slightly justified.
I was cleverly getting information out of them...
Snicker-Cleaver-ly.
You shut up!
Aside from extra hands being helpful,
You seem to have at least some knowledge on nobility, which is useful.

They don't even clean that good!!!
"Well,"
And what would we get out of this?
Yeah,
We're on a very important quest of true lo -mmhm-
Well, you'd get food, board,
And also the illusion of choice.
Consider it an exchange for lying to us.
You are PIRATES,
And why should we?

Well,
Seeing as you have only a small boat,
And, from the look of it, very few rations,
You'd be truly foolish not to stay until at least the next port.
Do that, plus a few chores here and there, we'll consider us even.
should you stay longer, we'll even help you deal with any emotional baggage you might have.
So what do you say?
Will you join of your own volition?
You said you'll help us?
Within reason.

Decisions don't need to be made right away.
But while you think about that, You can help with some chores.
It's not just me, right?
No, it's so rigged
Fine,
We accept your offer, and...
Apologise for that whole thing.
We promise to uphold our end if you do so yours.
That sounds like a fair deal,
Welcome aboard.

Would one of you do the introductions?
No.
Ugh.
Why.
Johann
Three fewer seats at dinner then?
Rock, Paper,
Piatră, hârtie,
じゃんけん
Scissors.
Foarfece.
じゃん けん！
My name is Shinju, you can call me Pearl.
Just for now, come to me if you're ill.
Why must you continue to fail me?
e one who atened you s Noemi.
Boy, I sure do wish I had some nice shoes for my poor, cold feet.
Oh, wait, I did.
The grumpy helmsman is Hopkin.
He's very secure in his masculinity, so feel free to poke fun at him as often as you possibly can.
Don't you FUCKING dare!
Then there's Johann, the cook.
Hours of entertainment.

Grigii is somewhere around here too.
And our esteemed captain Saga.
Keep your possessions close at all times, or else the little shit will put it in his nest.
Saga
Now then,
Your names, please.
Your real names, this time.

orte, short
r Fortunata

Jasper, not
short for
anything.

Well Forte,
Jasper,

It's lovely to
be acquainted
with you.

Only time
will tell if we
feel the same.

So
cynical.

Emi, can you
show them to
some empty
beds, thanks?

No.

Yeah,
I can...

And tomorrow, you
can show them how
to Griaii wrangle

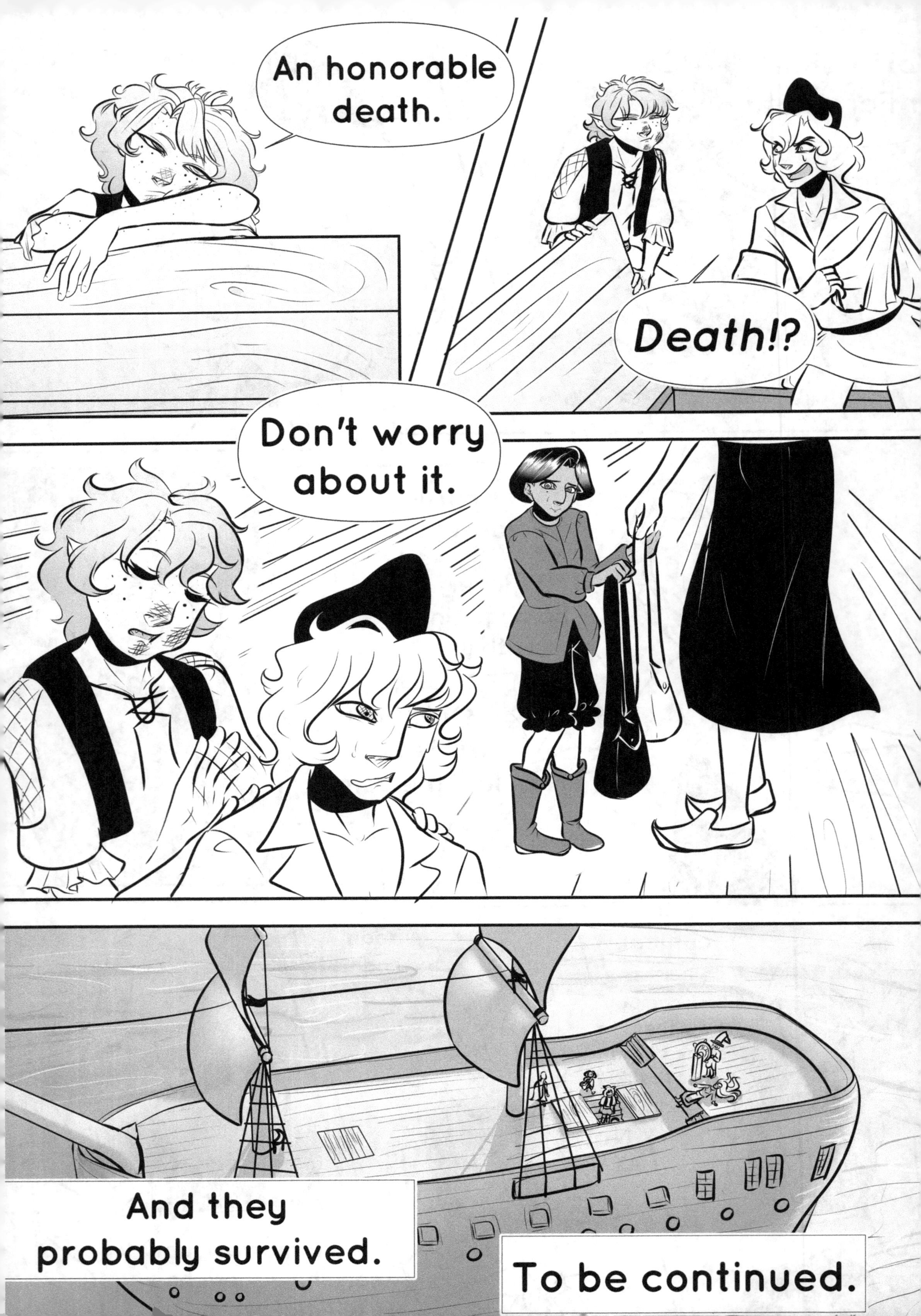
An honorable death.
Death!?
Don't worry about it.
And they probably survived.
To be continued.

Hi! Thank you for reading my book.
I really Appreciate It!
Speaking of thanks,

I'd like to thank these people for helping and supporting my crazy.
You know who you Are! Thank you guys so much!
Mom, Dad, Viking, Aunt, Friend, Sister

And to you, dear reader, I hope to see you next time.

Good Morrow!

Doodles

Pirates
Uncorrupted

As two young stowaways were
making their way to Mirth,
they are discovered by pirates.
These two drifters must figure
out how to survive long enough
to reach their destination.

Explore the world of Monte
through the eyes of Vampires,
Witches, Giants, Humans and
many others, as they try to
get by in their day-to-day
lives.